HALLY AND THE SIDEWAYS TOOTH

Written by NOAH P. FLESHER

Illustrated by JENNY CHEN

"Butterflies! Butterflies! We are Butterflies!"
For all the Butterflies!

PALMETTO
PUBLISHING

Charleston, SC
www.PalmettoPublishing.com

Paperback: 978-1-64990-349-5
Hardcover: 978-1-64990-104-0
eBook: 978-1-64990-348-8

Hally was a happy kindergartener
who always loved to learn and have fun.

She loved books and to read with a partner.

Hally loved to sketch and write
during writing workshop.
She had great friends and loved
to talk, learn and play with them.

She also liked events at school like ...

Halloween!

The 100th Day of School!

Earth Week!

And the Butterfly Café!

Like many kindergarteners, Hally lost her first tooth!

She was excited and took it home to show her parents.

That night, she left it
for you know who...

When Hally lost both her front teeth, her teacher Mr. Flesher joked and called her and other students in the Butterfly Class jack-o-lanterns!

Hally's first front tooth grew in, but it didn't look right.
It grew in sideways!

No one in the class teased her about her unique tooth, and Mr. Flesher told Hally it was neat and different.

Still, Hally felt a little embarrassed about her sideways tooth.

One day, Principal McTrout was getting some binder clips in the supply room. He got locked inside!

Ms. Twee, the head
secretary, came to the
Butterfly Classroom.

"Mr. Flesher, we need
help with a problem
in the office,"
she whispered.

Mr. Flesher called Hally over.

"Hally, I have an idea of how you can help solve this problem," he said.

15

16

Hally went to the office with Ms. Twee.

CLICK,

CLICK,

CLICK!

She picked the lock open with her sideways tooth in 20 seconds flat!

Principal McTrout thanked Hally for her help.

Hally returned to the Butterfly Class. As she entered the room, she felt proud.

She and Mr. Flesher exchanged a nod as Hally joined the class for the mini-lesson on the carpet.

Hally returned home after school. Her sister Celine, who was a big 5th grader, decided to make herself and Hally an afternoon snack. Tuna fish sandwiches. Hally loved tuna sandwiches!

As Celine began to open the can of tuna,
the can opener broke!

"Oh nooo, what are we going to do now?" Celine asked.

Hally looked at Celine.
"I can handle this! I'm a problem solver!"
she shouted.

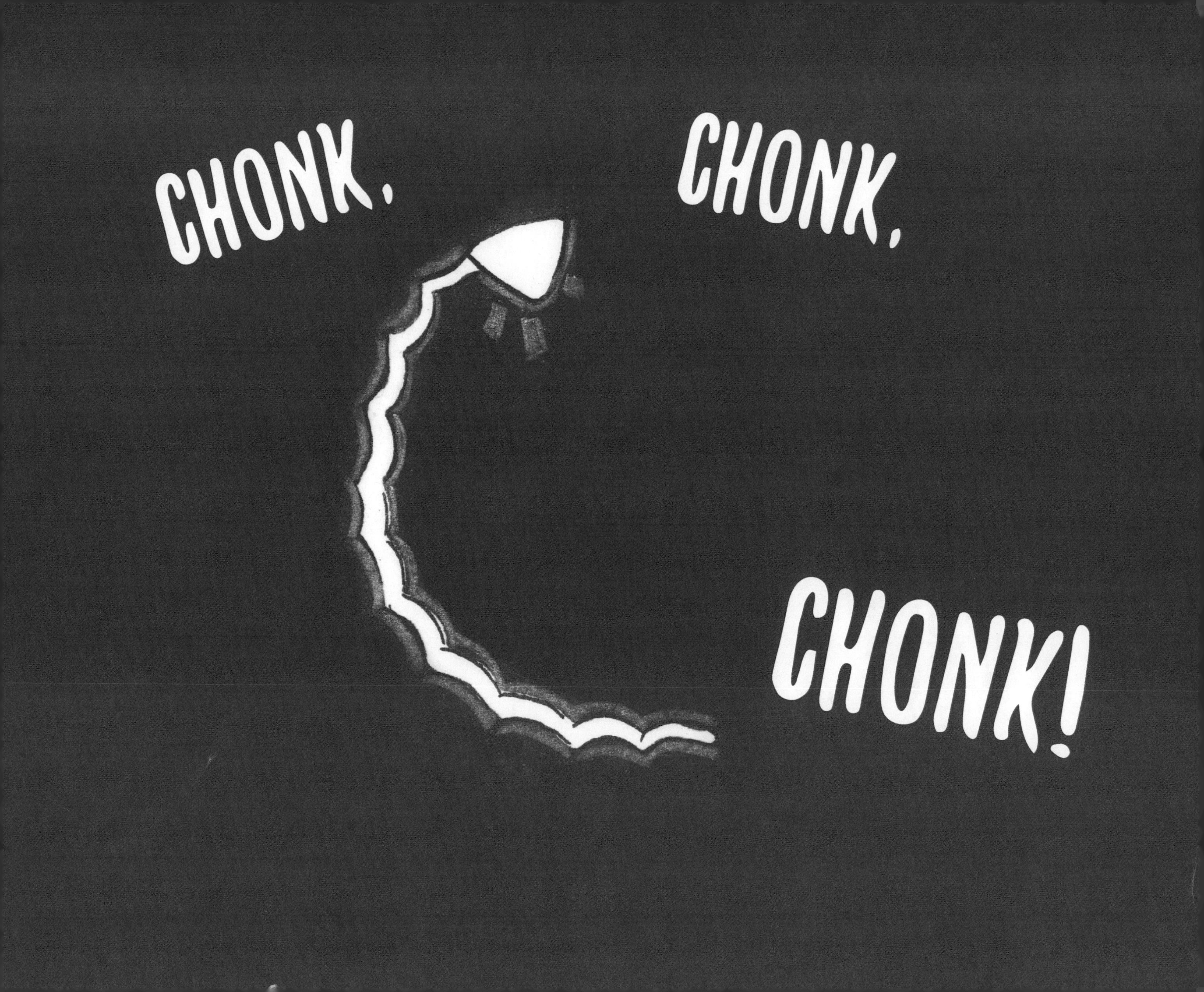
CHONK,
CHONK,
CHONK!

"Problem solved! Oh tuna la la!" said Hally.

She and Celine gave
each other a fist bump,
then enjoyed the tuna sandwiches.

During spring break, Hally and her family traveled by train for her cousin's wedding at the beach.

They arrived early to help
her cousins with the wedding.

Her Aunt Chung came over. "Oh no! The ice sculptor was on his way but is going to be very late.

He has a problem with his scooter. What are we going to do?" cried Aunt Chung.

Hally looked at Aunt Chung and shouted,
"I can handle this! I'm a problem solver!"

Hally returned to school and shared with the Butterflies and Mr. Flesher about the wedding events over spring break. She was very proud of being a problem solver!

Mr. Flesher exclaimed,
"I would like to compliment
Hally for being such a great
problem solver at school
and with her family!"

NOTES FOR TEACHERS AND PARENTS

Ms. Twee, the head secretary, came to the Butterfly Classroom.

"Mr. Flesher, we need help with a problem in the office," she whispered.

Her Aunt Chung came over. "Oh no! The ice sculptor was on his way but is going to be very late.

He has a problem with his scooter. What are we going to do?" cried Aunt Chung.

DIALOGUE

Quotation marks " " show a character's dialogue or talk.

In this book the color of the dialogue matches the clothing color of the character speaking. Ask your students or children, "Which character is talking on this page? What do you notice about the color of the letters and quotation marks? What connections can you make?"

Hally looked at Aunt Chung and shouted, "I can handle this! I'm a problem solver!"

Mr. Flesher exclaimed, "I would like to compliment Hally for being such a great problem solver at school and with her family!"

36

SOCIAL EMOTIONAL LEARNING (SEL) CONNECTIONS

Be a problem solver like Hally. Remember there are many ways to be creative and resourceful! Hally used her special tooth and creativity to solve problems in unexpected ways. In real life, we can also be creative, not give up, and be resourceful to solve problems. Sometimes we ask others to help us solve problems, too.

COMPLIMENTS

Mr. Flesher compliments Hally for being a problem solver at school and with her family! Remember the importance and power of giving and receiving compliments. Some examples are: "I love your creativity because …" "I want to compliment you for trying something new!" "I want to compliment you on being a problem solver!" Giving compliments encourages others, strengthens relationships and builds kindness. Descriptive compliments help build self-esteem, too.

ABOUT THE AUTHOR

NOAH P. FLESHER

Noah P. Flesher, Mr. Flesher, has been an international educator in Seoul, Saigon and Shanghai for over 20 years. His class is the Butterfly Class, and he has taught many "Butterflies" over the years in pre-kindergarten, kindergarten and first grade.

When he is not teaching, he spends time with Baker his chocolate poodle housemate. He currently spends school years in Shanghai and usually spends his summers at his old farm house in Midcoast Maine enjoying his woods, flowers and lily pond, and, of course, his friends.

ABOUT THE ILLUSTRATOR

JENNY CHEN

Jenny Chen is currently studying in college in Taipei, Taiwan. Art has always been a big part of Jenny's life, inspired by her older brother Louis.

She likes to observe the world around her. By doing so, she is able to combine her love of life and visual languages to create her own unique way of sharing emotions. Through her art, she gathers around her friends and family to create memorable moments.

ABOUT THEIR COLLABORATION

One day, Noah noticed some impressive illustrations Jenny shared online. He happened to be looking for an illustrator to illustrate his first picture book, *Hally and the Sideways Tooth*. Noah and Jenny began collaborating on the project. It took two and a half years to complete it amidst their busy lives.

Noah, Mr. Flesher, and Jenny had not worked together since 2003-2004 when Jenny was a Butterfly in his pre-kindergarten class in downtown Shanghai!

Mr. Flesher and the Butterfly Class - 2003

Jenny creating in the Butterfly Class - 2003

ABOUT HALLY

Hally is a real girl. She was in Mr. Flesher's Butterfly Class in Vietnam in 2012 when she really grew a sideways tooth!

While Hally is truly a problem solver in real life, *Hally and the Sideways Tooth*, veers into fun fiction. The real Hally didn't use her tooth to do all the amazing things fictional Hally does. Please don't try at home even with a sideways tooth.

Sometimes people have a tooth grow in sideways. It's called horizontal impaction. Hally saw a special tooth doctor called an orthodontist to help make her sideways tooth grow straight with braces.

CPSIA information can be obtained
at www.ICGtesting.com
Printed in the USA
BVRC091213210521
607789BV00010B/374